OWL & CAT

GO TO HAJJ

WORDS & PICTURES
BY EMMA APPLE

Little Moon Books – Dunedin, New Zealand

First Edition
Hardcover

ISBN-13: 978-0-473-48870-3

www.littlemoonbooks.com

OWL & CAT

GO TO HAJJ

Contents:

Introduction   – Page 5

Day 1   ■   – Page 11

Day 2   ■   – Page 25

Day 3   ■   – Page 37

Day 4   ■   – Page 57

Day 5   ■   – Page 63

Hajj is the pilgrimage to Mecca that every Muslim must make once in their lifetime. It starts on the 8th day of the Islamic month of Dhul-Hijjah and lasts for 5 days.

Owl and Cat are going to Mecca to show you what a pilgrim does on each of the 5 days of Hajj.

First, Owl and Cat pack their bags with everything they'll need during their hajj.

Then, Owl and Cat travel to Mecca.

DAY 1

On the first day of hajj
Owl and Cat change into special clothes.

This is called ihram.

On the first day of hajj
Owl and Cat walk around the
Kaaba 7 times.

This is called tawaf.

After tawaf, on the first day of hajj they walk between the two mountains, Safa and Marwa, 7 times.

This is called sa'iy.

On the morning of the first day of hajj Owl and Cat travel to the tent city of Mina.

On the first day of hajj

while they travel to Mina, they recite a prayer in Arabic called the Talbiya.

"Labbayk Allahumma Labbayk. Labbayk La Sharika Laka Labbayk. Innal-Hamda, Wa in-Ni'mata, Laka wal Mulk, La Sharika Lak."

"I am here, O Allah, I am here, there is no partner for You. I am here. Praise and glory is for You and The Kingdom is Yours. There is no partner for You."

The rest of the first day of hajj
is spent praying in Mina.

DAY 2

On the second day of hajj
Owl and Cat travel to the Arafat
desert plain.

On the second day of hajj
in Arafat, they stand in prayer at
Jabal ar-Rahma, The Mountain of
Mercy.

At sunset on the second day of hajj, Owl and Cat travel to a place called Muzdalifah to rest.

On the second day of hajj
at Muzdalifah they collect stones
to throw at pillars in Mina.

On the second day of hajj

many Muslims who are not on hajj

will fast.

DAY 3

Before sunrise on the third day of hajj,
Owl and Cat travel back to Mina.

On the third day of hajj
in Mina, they throw stones at pillars
called Jamarat.

On the third day of hajj,
Owl and Cat pay for the meat of
an animal to give to the needy.
This is called a sacrifice.

After the sacrifice, on the third day of hajj,

the men at hajj cut their hair.

On the third day of hajj,
Owl and Cat change out of ihram
into their normal clothes.

On the third day of hajj, they travel back to Mecca for the second tawaf, 7 times around the Kaaba.

After tawaf on the third day of hajj, they walk between the two mountains, Safa and Marwa, 7 times for the final sa'iy.

After sa'iy on the third day of hajj,
they travel back to the tent city in Mina.

The third day of hajj
is the beginning of Eid al-Adha, the
festival of the sacrifice.

Muslims around the world will
celebrate.

DAY 4

All of the fourth day of hajj
is spent in Mina.

On the fourth day of hajj,
they stone the jamarat pillars
again.

DAY 5

On the fifth day of hajj,
Owl and Cat stone the Jamarat
pillars in Mina one last time.

On the fifth day of hajj
they travel back to Mecca.

On the fifth day of hajj
they do the final tawaf, 7 times
around the Kaaba.

After tawaf on the fifth day of hajj,
Owl and Cat drink Zamzam water
from a special well in Mecca.

Their hajj is complete!
Hajj Mabroor, Owl and Cat!
We wish you a blessed and
accepted hajj!

THE

OWL & CAT

SERIES

The best-selling Owl & Cat picture book series helps children learn about the concepts of Friendship, Family, and Acceptance, with humor and an appeal that crosses the lines of culture and religion.

OTHER BOOKS IN THE OWL & CAT SERIES....

MORE FROM LITTLE MOON BOOKS

WHERE IS ALLAH?

CHILDREN'S FIRST QUESTIONS

Written & Illustrated by Emma Apple

WHAT'S THAT?

ما هذا؟

Maa haatha?

Written & Illustrated by Emma Apple

HOW BIG IS ALLAH?

CHILDREN'S FIRST QUESTIONS

Written & Illustrated by Emma Apple

One Meal More

A Multicultural Ramadan Story

by Emma Apple

LITTLE
MOON
BOOKS

littlemoonbooks.com